The Very Hairy Bear

Written by
Beth Shoshan

Illustrated by
Masumi Furukawa

PaRragon

Bath • New York • Singapore • Hong Kong • Cologne • Delhi
Melbourne • Amsterdam • Johannesburg • Auckland • Shenzhen

Here's a bear,
a Very Hairy Bear.

And here's a friend,
the Very Hairy Bear's best friend.

My House

Today, the Very
Hairy Bear
is wondering...

"What will I be
when I grow up?"

"Maybe," he thinks,
"I could be...

a warm, fluffy Panda Bear?"

"Or a cool and shimmering
Polar Bear!"

"Or maybe," thinks the
Very Hairy Bear, "I could be...

a gruff and grumpy Grizzly Bear?"

"Or a sweet
and sticky
Honey Bear!"

"Oh dear!" the Very Sticky Bear's best friend declares. "I've never seen a Flower Bear before!"

And now the Very Hairy Bear,
dressed like a Flowery Honey Bear,
has suddenly got lots and lots
of friends!

"Maybe," the Very Hairy
Bear yawns, "for now,
I"ll just be a bear...

a Very Hairy
Bear."

Here's a bear,
a Very Hairy Bear, in a
warm and soapy bath.

Hon

And here's a Very
Hairy Little Bear...

tucked up snug
in bed.

For Steph
- my best friend, my basherte,
my soulmate!

B.S.

For Yasushi & Micia

M.F.

This edition published by Parragon in 2012
Parragon
Queen Street House
4 Queen Street
Bath BA1 1HE, UK
www.parragon.com

Published by arrangement with Meadowside Children's Books
185 Fleet Street, London, EC4A 2HS

Text © Beth Shoshan 2011 Illustrations © Masumi Furukawa 2011

ISBN 978-1-4454-7231-7

Printed in China